Rock
of Ages

a tribute to the Black Church

Rock of Ages

By Tonya Bolden

Illustrated by
R. Gregory Christie

ALFRED A. KNOPF
NEW YORK

She plays Bach . . .
and the tambourine.

Her name is

Mother Zion Baptist All-Souls

Sanctified Rock Creek

A.M.E. Mount Mariah C.M.E. Marion

Avenue A.M.E.

Zion Church of the Good Shepherd

True Believers at the Cross

Straight Street Congregational

St. Mary's Lutheran

St. Peter's R.C.

St. Mark's Methodist

St. Philip's Presbyterian

Bethel Full-Gospel

Shiloh.

She has done so much

to make her people strong,

to keep so many alive in their bodies, in their souls.

Multitudes she has mothered

in times of dense distress.

When she was

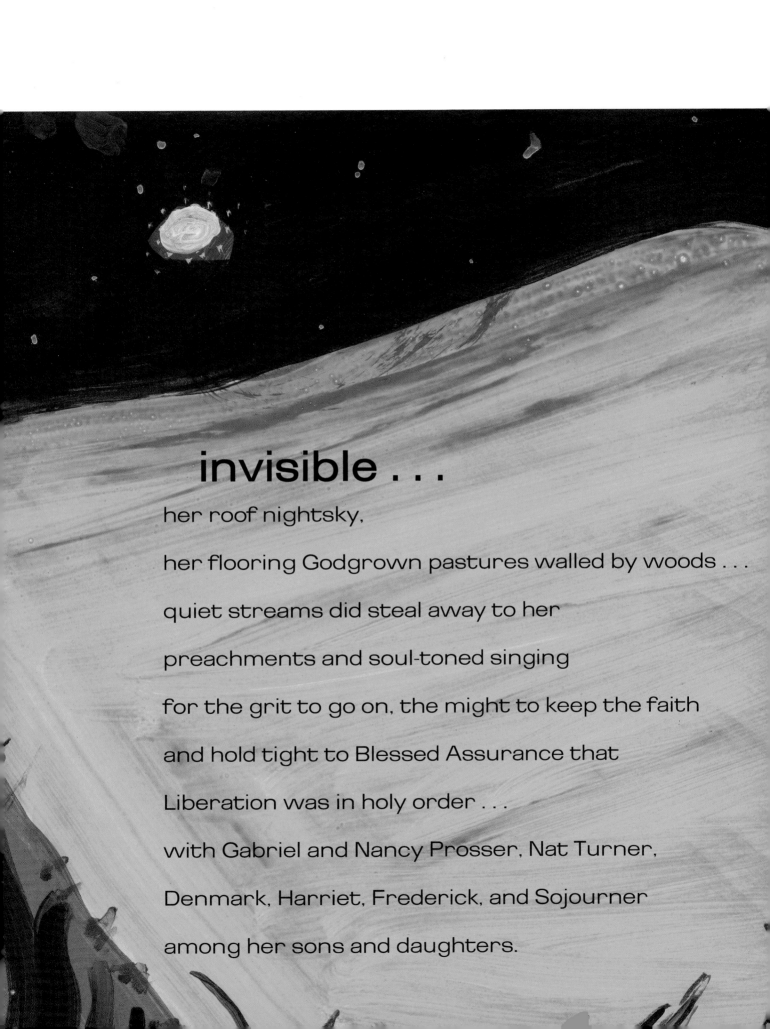

invisible . . .

her roof nightsky,

her flooring Godgrown pastures walled by woods . . .

quiet streams did steal away to her

preachments and soul-toned singing

for the grit to go on, the might to keep the faith

and hold tight to Blessed Assurance that

Liberation was in holy order . . .

with Gabriel and Nancy Prosser, Nat Turner,

Denmark, Harriet, Frederick, and Sojourner

among her sons and daughters.

When she came to be seen . . .

in timber,

in brick,

in stone—

she remained a refuge of resistance

where the 'buked and scorned assembled

to be renewed in the spirit to be fortified in the

mind to help themselves heal, stand up, stand

tall.

Wasn't it she who raised in singles
and change much money

for raising schools, associations, old folks' homes,

for doing

doing
doing:

when the Thompson family got burned out,

when Brother Payne passed and his widow had no mite,

when Sister Mayhew took sick,

when badbutt Jasper was hungry?

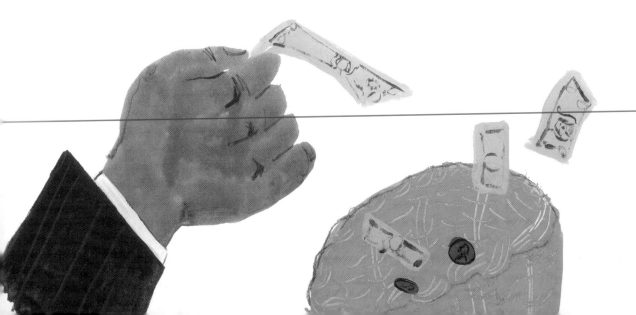

When we were the **not-alloweds**

and **go-to-the-back-door** people,

she was a warm place to be

treasurer,

trustee,

M.C.

Cradle, too, was she for

creative fire:

where Aretha, Leontyne, Sam, Dinah, Della

first found voice,

where Brother Baldwin laid hands on rhythms

he worked with words,

where Martin learned to speak.

Most everywhere her
pastors, preachers, elders, evangelists,

the business board, the deacons—men,

with troops of women

piloting pageants, corralling committees,

women frying the chicken, crying with the sick,

women taking girls and boys to Sunday School

to learn basic Bible stories and about the Lord and

to sit up straight and not fidget . . .

women encouraging slackers to buck up and get

dignity with

their mere presence in Sunday Best . . .

those marvelous hats, neat shoes, pressed dresses,

pocketbooks never without handkerchief and

peppermint balls . . .

women gathering in prayer bands to war against

woes and wrongs.

She lives in cathedralettes, in city-brick with faux stained glass,

in stubby storefronts,

in clapboard A-frames

in Fayette,

Philly,

New York City,

Kansas City,

Kannapolis,

Indianapolis,

Damascus,

Columbus,

Birmingham,

Baltimore,

Boston,

Austin,

Laurel,

Greenwood,

Asheville,

Nashville,

Nazareth. . . .

Arms ever-always open . . .

through the neglect and disrespect,

lack, attacks,

ashes . . .

to embrace the children

of her children's children

and their child

to be born.

Notes

She plays Bach . . . and the tambourine.

Singing and music have always been a large part of the Black Church, and there are several different styles associated with it. There are spirituals, which arose during the time of slavery and were rooted in African chants, moans, and field hollers. Other styles include gospel and even "sacred rap." Everyone sings in the Black Church, though not necessarily at the same time: there are choirs, ensembles, quintets, quartets, trios, duets, and soloists, and sometimes the entire congregation joins in raising their voices. They may sing a cappella or accompanied by grand organs, upright pianos, baby grands, saxophones,

trombones and other brass, guitars (both electric and acoustic), drums (all kinds), a shekere (a rattle made from a gourd), or even just a washboard or woodblocks or a plain old tambourine to keep the beat.

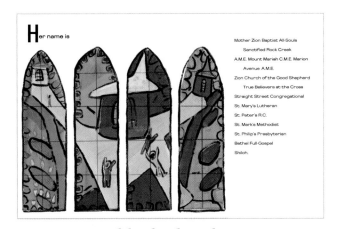

Her name is Mother Zion Baptist All-Souls Sanctified Rock Creek A.M.E. Mount Mariah C.M.E. Marion Avenue A.M.E. Zion Church of the Good Shepherd True Believers at the Cross Straight Street Congregational St. Mary's Lutheran St. Peter's R.C. St. Mark's Methodist St. Philip's Presbyterian Bethel Full-Gospel Shiloh.

The majority of black churches are Baptist, and the second-highest number of congregations are Pentecostal (also called Holiness or Sanctified). Other denominations include the African Methodist Episcopal (A.M.E.) Church, the African Methodist Episcopal Zion (A.M.E. Zion) Church, and the Christian Methodist Episcopal (C.M.E.) Church (originally the Colored Methodist Episcopal Church when established in 1870). What's more, you will find black congregations that are Adventist, Congregational, Roman Catholic, Lutheran, Presbyterian, Episcopalian, African Orthodox, and non-denominational.

During the days of slavery, some Christian slaveholders provided religious instruction to their captives. Other slaveholders did not allow their enslaved people to practice Christianity—the very idea of a black Christian offended them—so those slaves turned to secret teaching/preaching and Bible reading, frequently in fields at night. When these "invisible churches" were discovered, their congregants were often severely punished. Churches formed by free blacks were sometimes targets for violence by those who were threatened by blacks organizing together.

Many of the nineteenth-century freedom fighters were Christians. There were Gabriel and Nancy Prosser, co-leaders of a spoiled uprising in 1800 in Henrico County, Virginia: both husband and wife were Baptists, and Gabriel was a preacher. There was the freedman Denmark Vesey, who, in the winter of 1821 in a church outside Charleston, South Carolina, laid plans for a revolt the following summer. In the summer of 1831, Nat Turner, a Baptist preacher, captained an uprising in Southampton County, Virginia. The long list of black Christian abolitionists also includes the once enslaved Frederick Douglass, Sojourner Truth, and Harriet Tubman; the freeborn scholar Alexander Crummell; entrepreneur James Forten; minister Henry Highland Garnet; and writers Frances Ellen Watkins Harper and Maria W. Stewart.

The oldest continuously operating black church in America is in Savannah, Georgia: First African Baptist Church, formed in the late 1770s. One of the fine footnotes of First African Baptist's history is that it was there (at 23 Montgomery Street) that several months before the March on Washington, Martin Luther King, Jr. first delivered his "I Have a Dream" speech.

Perhaps the most famous early black church is Bethel Church in Philadelphia, Pennsylvania, founded in 1794 by the freedman Richard Allen (1760–1831) after his previous church adopted segregated seating. Bethel is known as the "mother" (or founding) church of the African Methodist Episcopal denomination.

As the nineteenth century moved on, out of love and protest, the number of black churches grew, greatly increasing after the abolition of slavery (in 1865). In 1890, there were approximately 19,000 black churches. By 1906, that number had almost doubled. At the end of the twentieth century, there were upwards of 60,000 black churches, some with only a few dozen members and others with thousands.

Wasn't it she who raised in singles
and change much money

for raising schools, associations, old folks' homes,

for doing

doing
doing:

when the Thompson family got burned out,
when Brother Payne passed and his widow had no mite,
when Sister Mayhew took sick,
when badbutt Jasper was hungry?

From its infancy and throughout its growth, following the traditions of Christian charity and black self-help, the Black Church has been black America's number-one social service agency. With schools (sheltering some, erecting some, supporting others), housing for senior citizens, job clinics, scholarships for the college-bound, day care, after-school programs, low-cost hearty meals, food banks, clothing banks, burial money, and other emergency aid, it has supported its communities in many ways.

Cradle, too, was she for

creative fire:

where Aretha, Leontyne, Sam, Dinah, Della
first found voice.
where Brother Baldwin laid hands on rhythms
he worked with words.
where Martin learned to speak.

Scores of young singers and musicians got their start and main training in a church band or choir. While many also studied music and voice elsewhere, the church was the place that most welcomed their talents and gave them the most opportunities to refine their craft.

Among the many well-known artists owing much to the Black Church have been Marian Anderson, Anita Baker, Sam Cooke, Al Green, Gladys Knight, Leontyne Price, Lou Rawls, Bernice Johnson Reagon, Della Reese, Dinah Washington, and (of course) "the Queen of Soul," Aretha Franklin, and "the Godfather of Soul," James Brown. Much of black literature has been influenced by the Black Church, its culture and its ways of worship. James Baldwin's *Go Tell It on the Mountain* is one famous example. As well, many of America's finest orators have come out of the Black Church. Among the most remembered is Martin Luther King, Jr.

Arms ever-always open . . .
through the neglect and disrespect,
lack, attacks,
ashes . . .
to embrace the children
of her children's children
and their child
to be born.

One of the Black Church's greatest sorrows came at the end of the twentieth century—fire. Between 1995 and 1998, upwards of 500 black churches were totally or partially ruined by flames (with the majority of these church burnings occurring in the South). Most grievous of all is that so many of these fires were acts of arson, many racially motivated.

Author's Note

Several years ago, in the midst of a casual, meandering conversation about black life and history in America, my friend and fellow writer Elza Dinwiddie-Boyd remarked, "If you don't know about the Black Church, you don't know about the black experience." This crisp, shining truth was partial inspiration for *Rock of Ages.*

To be sure, regardless of your religion, if you have any interest in American history, you cannot overlook the role that the Black Church has played in black survival and triumphs.

Rock of Ages was a work in progress (in my heart) years before Elza's incisive comment. As a "child" of the Black Church, with the overwhelming majority of my friends and relatives members, I knew without being told what a sustainer and provider this institution was for my people. (Indeed, it was principally in church that I learned leadership skills, as well as to "sit up straight and not fidget." Church was where I was exposed to some of the most soulful music in the world, and where I savored the best ever penny-a-piece peppermint balls, slipped to me out of the pocketbook of my mother, or an aunt, or some kind Sister So-and-So.) As a youngster in the 1960s, I also knew—again only intuitively—that it was in the Black Church that my people could lay down their racial burdens—could be safe and free from the covert and overt indignities and hostilities they experienced. So, yes, early on I knew the Black Church was, in so many ways, a lifeline, a lifesaver.

But it often takes the brain a while to catch up with the heart.

The "supporting evidence" for the historical significance and power of the Black Church mounted up over the years. For instance, while researching for an essay about the "Father of Black History," Carter G. Woodson, I inevitably came across his book *The History of the Negro Church* (1921). Over time, my permanent collection would come to include such titles as *The Negro Church in America* by E. Franklin Frazier, *Frustrated Fellowship: The Black Baptist Quest for Social Power* by James Melvin Washington, *The Black Church in the African American Experience* by C. Eric Lincoln and Lawrence H. Mamiya, and *Out of the Ashes: Burned Churches and the Community of Faith,* edited by Norman A. Hjelm.

Time and again, I discovered that yet another grand activist or educator or leader in some other field was a minister or faithful church member. Time and again, I discovered that yet another celebrated artist or writer or singer had been "mothered" by the Black Church. Of course, we can never forget that during the civil rights movement of the 1950s and 1960s, so often it was in the basements and sanctuaries of black churches that people were organized and educated on the movement, that boycotts and demonstrations were planned, that the plate was passed for the funding of so much civil rights work, that demonstrators were fed or had their wounds bound up following attacks by segregationists. Thus each new discovery about the creations, the work, the monumental presence of this institution in my people's lives moved me closer and closer to turning some of my God-given talent to a small tribute to the Black Church.

Text copyright © 2001 by Tonya Bolden
Illustrations copyright © 2001 by R. Gregory Christie
All rights reserved under International and Pan-American Copyright Conventions. Published in the United States
of America by Alfred A. Knopf, a division of Random House, Inc., New York, and simultaneously in Canada by
Random House of Canada Limited, Toronto. Distributed by Random House, Inc., New York.

KNOPF, BORZOI BOOKS, and the colophon are registered trademarks of Random House, Inc.

The poem "Rock of Ages" appeared in a slightly different version in *In Praise of Our Fathers and Our Mothers:
A Black Family Treasury by Outstanding Authors and Artists,* compiled by Wade Hudson and Cheryl Willis Hudson
(Just Us Books, 1997).

www.randomhouse.com/kids

Library of Congress Cataloging-in-Publication Data
Bolden, Tonya.
Rock of ages / by Tonya Bolden ; illustrated by R. Gregory Christie.—1st ed.
p.   cm.
Summary: A poem celebrating the role of the church in the lives and history of African Americans, from the time of
slavery through the struggle for civil rights to the well-established churches of today.
ISBN 0-679-89485-3 (trade)
ISBN 0-679-99485-8 (lib. bdg.)
1. African American churches—Juvenile poetry. 2. African Americans—Religion—Juvenile poetry.
3. Children's poetry, American. [1. African American churches—Poetry. 2. African Americans—Religious life—
Poetry. 3. American poetry.] I. Christie, R. Gregory, 1971–ill. II. Title.

PS3552.O5828 R63 2001
811'.54—dc21
          2001038534

Printed in the United States of America
December 2001
10 9 8 7 6 5 4 3 2
First Edition

For Simon Boughton, who "gets it."

—T.B.

For the St. Amant, Jean-Pierre,
Foster, and Myer families.
Once again I see what those
mandatory Sunday sessions
were all about.

— R.G.C.